★ American

forever friends

Madison's New Buddy

★ American Girl®

forever friends

Madison's New Buddy

🐾 By Crystal Velasquez 🐾

SCHOLASTIC INC.

Published by Scholastic Inc., *Publishers since 1920.* SCHOLASTIC and associated logos are trademarks and/or registered trademarks of Scholastic Inc. The publisher does not have any control over and does not assume any responsibility for author or third-party websites or their content.

This book is a work of fiction. Names, characters, places, and incidents are either the product of the author's imagination or are used fictitiously, and any resemblance to actual persons, living or dead, business establishments, events, or locales is entirely coincidental.

Book design by Yaffa Jaskoll

ISBN 978-1-338-11493-5

10 9 8 7 6 5 4 3 2 1   18 19 20 21 22

Printed in the U.S.A.   23

First printing 2018

To Blossom—my favorite canine houseguest. You make pet sitting fun.

C.V.

❀Table of Contents❀

Madison Rosen twirled in front of the mirror in her room, her copper-colored hair fanning out around her. Bright yellow baby chicks dotted her skirt, there was a Labrador retriever puppy on her T-shirt, and she was wearing the kitten charm necklace from her new friends Jasmine Arroyo, Keiko Hayashi, and Sofia Davis. No doubt about it, she had on the very best outfit for the ribbon-cutting ceremony and grand reopening of Rosa's Refuge Animal Shelter.

"Honey, hurry up!" her mother called. "We don't want to be late."

"Coming, Mom," Madison shouted as she ran down the stairs.

She walked into the kitchen to find her two cats, Leo and Pepper, rubbing themselves against her mom's ankles and meowing with all their might.

Her mother laughed softly. "Lunch will be ready in a second," she told the cats. "Hold your horses."

"They're always hungry," Madison said with a giggle. Whenever she opened a can of cat food, the kittens came running as if they hadn't eaten in weeks. That was probably why they'd grown so much since Madison brought them home. They almost didn't look like kittens anymore. Soon they would be full-grown cats! Leo and Pepper had made it easier for Madison to move to a new house, and Madison was glad her mother had agreed to adopt them.

Her mom put the bowls of food and water on the floor, then stood back as the cats attacked their lunch, dipping their furry heads into their dishes, "That ought to hold them for a while," she said. "Ready, Maddie?"

Madison flew to the door, holding it open and bouncing up and down.

"Yes!" she cried excitedly. "Let's go!"

When Madison and her mother reached the animal shelter, there was already a large crowd out front. Among their neighbors, Madison

3

spotted the school principal, Mr. Brady, and her friends Jasmine, Keiko, and Sofia. While her mother went to say hello to Jasmine's mother, who was a vet at the animal shelter, Madison joined her friends near the front of the crowd.

"Hi, guys!" she greeted them. "Did I miss anything?"

"Not yet," Jasmine said. "You're just in time."

Mrs. Wallace, the director of the shelter, appeared under the arch of colorful balloons and the blue banner that said GRAND REOPENING! Beside them a red ribbon stretched in front of the wide double doors.

"Thank you so much for coming!" Mrs. Wallace greeted the crowd warmly.

Everyone cheered.

"Because of you, the shelter is bigger and better than ever, and we can help a lot more animals in need," Mrs. Wallace said. She picked up a giant pair of scissors and snipped the ribbon. "Rosa's Refuge Animal Shelter is open . . . again!"

The shelter was now twice the size it had been, thanks to the money Madison and her friends had helped raise a few months ago. Now that Madison and her mom had officially moved to town, she could spend a lot more time volunteering there.

Madison and her friends clapped and cheered. Then they followed the small crowd inside to celebrate with cookies and lemonade. The new shelter was even more beautiful than Madison had imagined. The walls were a soft baby blue, there was a play area in the back, and there were rows of brand-new cages right in front, most of them filled with dogs.

The girls ran to the nearest cages. A scruffy-looking terrier pawed at the thin metal bars. Next to him, a border collie and a beagle puppy were yipping and whining as they paced back and forth in their cages. At the end of the row, a golden retriever puppy sat in the middle of his cage with his nose nuzzled between his paws and his eyes droopy and sad. As Madison watched, the school principal tried to greet him.

"Hey, little guy," Mr. Brady said, reaching one finger between the bars to try to stroke the puppy's fur. But the dog crept away from him. He moved to the back of the cage and shivered in fear, his tail tucked between his legs.

"Aw, he looks scared," Madison said to Jasmine. "I wonder what's wrong with him."

"I don't know," Jasmine replied, concerned. "Let's ask Mrs. Wallace."

The girls waved Mrs. Wallace over. She peered sadly at the nervous pup. "Buddy was rescued from a home where he was being neglected. I think he's still nervous around people. A lot of the new arrivals are skittish and need time to become used to being handled so that they can be adopted."

"Is there anything we can do for him?" Madison asked.

Mrs. Wallace looked thoughtful. "I'm not sure," she replied. "But animals are a lot like people. They're social creatures, and just being around volunteers like you girls will help. Most dogs relax as they become more comfortable in their new environment."

"It's a little like starting at a new school," Mr. Brady added with a kind smile at Madison.

Madison peered into the golden retriever's cage again, heartbroken at how sad he looked. "Don't worry," she whispered. "You're safe here. And I'm going to do whatever I can to help you."

"We all will," Jasmine agreed, throwing her arm around Madison's shoulder and giving her friend a big smile. "Maybe we can come up with ways to help the dogs relax. When I'm sad or upset, I know I like to sit in a bubble bath and read a favorite book."

"Drawing or painting makes me feel better when I'm down," Keiko added.

"Music helps me relax," Sofia said thoughtfully.

"So we just have to figure out a way to teach these dogs to read, paint, or play an instrument," Madison joked playfully.

"Actually, that's a great idea, Madison!" Jasmine replied. "We could read to the dogs! Our teachers want us to practice reading, right, Mr. Brady? We're always doing partner reading in school. We could do partner reading here, but with dogs! Wouldn't that be fun?"

"That's a great idea!" Keiko said.

"Yeah, I love it," Sofia agreed.

Madison's heart sank. Partner reading was her least favorite thing to do at school.

The truth was, she had trouble reading. It seemed to be so easy for everyone else, but not

for her. She had been seeing a reading specialist, Ms. Patel, ever since she transferred into
the school, and she'd made some progress.
But it still took her a long time to read even
one page.

"Um, yeah," Madison said quietly.
"Great idea."

Now Buddy wasn't the only one who was
anxious and uncomfortable. Madison knew
exactly how he felt.

Chapter 2:
School Surprise

Madison had thought being the new girl at school would be scary. But knowing Jasmine, Sofia, and Keiko had made it much easier. Now that Madison had been there a few weeks, she was settling in.

"I still can't believe we're all in the same class," Jasmine said, taking the seat next to Madison's and pulling out her notebook.

"Me neither," said Madison. "I was so

nervous about starting school here, but now I just feel lucky to have you all in my class!"

Still, Madison wasn't entirely comfortable at school, especially when it came to partner reading. So far, the class had only done it a few times, but their teacher, Ms. Chu, was always talking about it. It seemed like it was only a matter of time before everyone knew Madison's secret.

Ms. Chu finished taking attendance and began handing out sheets of paper. "Now, class, you'll all remember that last week we had visitors come in for Career Day. They each told us who, or what, inspired them. For the next few weeks, we'll be talking about inspiration. Your final project will be to write about someone who inspires you."

"Can we write about anybody?" Eddie Temple blurted out.

Ms. Chu nodded her head patiently. "Yes, anyone you'd like. But I'm handing out a list of suggestions in case you need ideas."

Everyone started buzzing about who they would pick.

Madison thought of all the famous people from history she admired, like Amelia Earhart, Martin Luther King Jr., and Abraham Lincoln. *Or maybe I'll choose someone who loves animals, like the scientist Jane Goodall.* Madison knew she had studied chimpanzees in the wild.

"Well, you have plenty of time to decide," Ms. Chu said, interrupting Madison's thoughts as she returned to the front of the room. "In a few weeks, you will all read your writing out loud to the class."

Suddenly, Madison's excitement faded. "Read . . . out loud?" she whispered.

But Ms. Chu wasn't done. "In addition to the essay," she continued, "the entire grade will be participating in a new program—the Shelter Dog Reading Project!"

"Are we really going to teach dogs to read?" David Bishop asked. "Cool!"

Everyone giggled.

"Not quite," Ms. Chu replied with a grin. "You'll be reading *to* the dogs. Many of the rescued animals are nervous in their new surroundings. The idea is that the sound of someone reading to them will help them relax and make them more comfortable around people."

She walked to her desk and picked up a piece of paper. "I know some of you already volunteer at the shelter," she said, smiling at Madison, Jasmine, Keiko, and Sofia. "But with so many animals to tend to, they'll need a lot more readers. Our own Jasmine Arroyo had the idea to make this a grade-wide project."

Madison glanced over at Jasmine. Her friend was beaming. She looked so excited. But Madison still felt as anxious about the project as she had when Jasmine first had the idea.

"It's a volunteer assignment," Ms. Chu continued. "Whoever would like to can sign up. But I encourage you all to take part if you can."

Madison sighed. It was bad enough that she would have to read out loud in front of her class at school. Now she was going to have to do it at the shelter, too! What if the other kids laughed at her when they heard her slowly sounding out the words and getting some of them wrong? The shelter was one of Madison's favorite places, but now she knew she would be worried and anxious whenever she was there.

"In addition to helping the animals, this program will provide extra practice reading for all of you, which is always a good thing." Ms. Chu fastened the sheet of paper to the dry-erase board at the front of the room. "If you want to participate, please sign this sheet." Immediately, several kids sprang up from their chairs to add their names.

Jasmine turned to Madison and squealed. "This is going to be awesome! We can sign up together."

"I don't know," Madison said, biting her lip. Maybe she could come up with a way out of it. "I have so much work to do. I mean, what about school? And the writing assignment? I'll need to find someone to write about. I might have to do research at the library."

"You can do both at the same time," Keiko said. "Check out some biographies of famous people from the library and read them to the dogs. It's perfect!"

"Yeah," Sofia agreed enthusiastically.

Madison looked helplessly at the line of kids waiting to add their names to the sign-up sheet. "Yes, but it looks like there will be so many volunteers already. They probably don't need me, too."

Principal Brady appeared at the door, tugging at the knot on his navy-blue tie. "Good morning, Ms. Chu," he said. "I see you've already told your class about the reading project."

A few kids cried out, "Yeah!" and Eddie pumped his fist.

Mr. Brady laughed and clapped his large hands together. "Wonderful! I'm glad to see so many of you want to pitch in. In fact, I dropped by to let you know that the class with the most volunteers is going to get a prize: a pizza party!"

Everyone went wild with cheers. Jasmine turned to Madison. "Did you hear that? The more people we have sign up, the closer we are to a pizza party. This is going to be great!"

Madison sighed as she watched her friends make their way to the sign-up sheet. She was fresh out of excuses. If she backed out now, she wouldn't just be letting Jasmine and her other friends and the animals down, she'd be disappointing her entire class. So she slowly rose from her chair and joined the line, wondering how she was going to keep the truth hidden from her friends.

Chapter 3:
A Stressful Secret

That Saturday, Madison met her friends at the animal shelter as usual. They were in the new grooming area, helping Mrs. Wallace wash a Shetland sheepdog named Bandit. He hated baths, but he loved getting dry. Right then, he was pushing his small head into the towel and shimmying his whole body, trying to shake every last drop of water away.

Mrs. Wallace handed Madison a flat brush.

"Would you like to do the honors?" she asked.

"Sure!" Madison said eagerly. She loved grooming Bandit. Madison pulled the brush gently through the dog's long black-and-brown hair.

"There you go," Madison said to the dog softly as she brushed. "This will keep your fur from getting matted. You don't want to look like Stella did when she first arrived here, do you?"

Madison tilted her head toward the fuzzy-looking black creature Sofia was holding.

"What breed is Stella again?" Keiko wondered.

"Stella is a Chow Chow," said Mrs. Wallace,

"but we couldn't even tell when she first came in since she'd been left out in the rain and her hair was lying flat. But now . . ."

Stella's hair poofed out in every direction, her dark beady eyes almost disappearing in a sea of fur along with her tiny ears. If Stella hadn't been panting and sniffing at Sofia's face with her wet nose, Madison would have thought she was a stuffed animal.

"Now she's gorgeous!" Keiko cried. "I'd love to have a coat that pretty. I mean, if I were a dog. She'll get adopted in no time."

"Yeah, by me," Sofia said hopefully, cuddling the Chow Chow even closer. Sofia was still trying hard to convince her parents that she was responsible enough to have a dog.

Jasmine's mother, Dr. Arroyo, entered the room and let out a laugh. "Maybe, Sofia, maybe. But for now, Stella has an appointment with me." She held out her arms.

Sofia sighed and handed Stella over to Jasmine's mom, who brushed the dog's hair back with her fingers.

"Now, let's go examine those ears," Dr. Arroyo said soothingly.

"Good luck finding them!" Sofia called after her.

"Have you guys decided what book you're going to read to the dogs yet?" Jasmine asked. She took off a pair of big yellow rubber gloves and set them on the side of the sink.

At the mention of the reading project,

Madison sank a little on her stool. Somehow she hadn't thought about it at all since she had arrived at the shelter.

"Not yet," Keiko said. "I might go with *Charlotte's Web*, though the ending is a little sad."

"I was thinking about *Shiloh*," Sofia added.

"That would be a good choice," Jasmine replied thoughtfully. "I haven't decided yet, but *Because of Winn-Dixie* might be nice. I love that book."

The girls went back and forth for a while, naming some of their favorites. Finally, Keiko turned to Madison.

"What about you?" she asked. "Have you picked a book yet?"

Madison shook her head and silently focused

on brushing Bandit's hair. Her cheeks turned red with embarrassment as she thought about her friends learning her secret. What was she going to do? Bandit seemed to notice how distracted she was because he began to wiggle and squirm. Madison made him sit so she could reach the patch of white on his chest.

"If you need help picking a book, we can all go with you to the library and help you find a good one," Jasmine suggested when she noticed how quiet Madison was. "Then we can take turns reading to each other to see how it sounds!"

But Sofia shook her head. "We can't read out loud in the library. We have to be quiet as mice in there. Have you ever been shushed by the librarian?" She shuddered. "It's super embarrassing. I can't think of anything worse."

Madison could. She pictured standing in front of the kids from school, reading, while they all pointed and laughed.

"Madison, are you okay?" Jasmine asked. "You don't seem like yourself."

"I'm fine," she answered quickly. "I'm just not feeling well, I guess. My stomach is a little queasy."

"Oh no," said Jasmine, biting her lip. "Maybe you should let my mom examine you."

"She's not a cat, Jaz," Sofia pointed out with a laugh. "I doubt Madison is about to cough up a hair ball."

Madison handed Jasmine the brush and rose from her seat. "Thanks, guys, but I think maybe I just need some water," she said. "I'll be right back."

She hurried out of the room and took her time making her way to the water cooler in the kitchen. Keeping this secret from her friends was going to be harder than she thought.

Chapter 4:
Friendship Advice

When school let out, Madison followed the crowd to the exit, dragging her feet the whole way. The Shelter Dog Reading Project was beginning tomorrow, and everyone was so excited about it that they had talked about it all day. Everyone except Madison, that is.

She was relieved to see her mom waiting for her. Madison ran into her arms and hugged her tightly.

"Wow!" said her mom, warmly squeezing her back. "I'm glad to see you, too!"

"Thanks," Madison said.

"Rough day at school?" her mom guessed as she put her arm around Madison's shoulders and started walking toward home. Her mom always seemed to know when something was bothering her.

Madison nodded. "Everyone keeps talking about the reading project at the shelter. But I'm not ready to read in front of anyone. I don't know what to do."

"You'll be there with your friends," her mother said. "I'm sure the girls understand."

Madison shifted her eyes away guiltily. "Um . . . actually, I haven't told them yet."

Her mom stopped walking and turned to face Madison. "You must be very anxious, then," her mom said sympathetically. "Why not?"

"I don't know," Madison mumbled. "I think I'm afraid of what they'll think."

Madison's mother squeezed her shoulder as they continued to walk down the tree-lined block that led to their new house. "I think your new friends will be supportive, don't you?"

Madison shrugged. "I don't know," she said nervously.

Her mother studied her quietly for a moment. "Do you want me to talk to your teacher?" she asked. "If you're that nervous about the volunteer reading project, I could explain the situation and let her know you won't be participating."

Madison stared up at her mom, her round grayish-blue eyes wide and serious. "I can't back out," she said. "The project was Jasmine's idea. And the class with the most volunteers wins a pizza party. Jasmine, Keiko, and Sofia are counting on me, and they're all convinced we're going to win the party. I don't want to be the reason we lose."

Her mother nodded slowly. "I see." By then, they had arrived home. Madison's mom sat on the top step of the porch and patted the spot beside her. Madison plopped down and leaned into her mom's comforting hug. She couldn't help letting a few tears slide down her face.

"Well then," her mother said, "why not trust your friends with the truth? Tell them reading is a struggle for you, but you're working with a specialist to get better."

"Mom, no!" Madison gasped. "I'd be so embarrassed."

Her mom squeezed her shoulder. "Honey, there's nothing for you to be ashamed of. You've worked so hard, and you've come such a long way already. Soon you'll be reading just as well as anyone in the class. In the meantime, you could use your friends' support."

Madison sniffled and raised her head to look at her mom. "But what if they make fun of me? What if they don't want to be my friends anymore?"

"I don't think they'd do that," said her mother. "But if they do, they aren't real friends anyway."

Madison knew her mother was right. But would her best friends still be there for her once they knew the truth?

When Madison woke the next morning, she felt a little better. She vowed to take her mom's advice and tell her friends the truth as soon as she saw them that morning. But first she had to get ready for school. And she had to choose a few books to bring to read at the shelter that day, too.

Madison went over to the bookshelf in the corner of her freshly painted yellow room. There were a few books right on top that her mom had been reading to her at night before bed. She picked up *Bunnicula*, a really funny story about a vampire rabbit. The narrator was actually a dog! It would be the perfect choice for the reading project. But it wouldn't be an easy book for Madison to read aloud on her own.

She sighed. All of the books on her shelf were books she and her mom read together. But then Madison noticed a few books on the bottom shelf that she hadn't read in ages. She saw *The Cat in the Hat* and *Green Eggs and Ham,* which had been her favorite Dr. Seuss books when she first learned how to read. In fact, she had loved them so much that she knew all the words by heart.

That's it! Madison thought suddenly, as she grabbed the two books and slipped them into her backpack. She wouldn't have to read these at all—she could just say the words from memory! Then she wouldn't even have to worry about telling her friends about her reading problem.

"Madison?" her mom called from downstairs. "Time for breakfast!"

"Coming, Mom!" Madison shouted back. She still wasn't looking forward to the reading project, but at least now she had a plan for getting through it.

Chapter 5:
A Lucky Day

As the yellow school bus pulled into the animal shelter parking lot, Jasmine pressed her hands against the windows, tapping excitedly on the glass. "We're here! We're finally here!" she shouted, her brown corkscrew curls bouncing along with her.

Sofia, who was sitting next to Jasmine, winced. "Ouch! You're going to burst my eardrum, Arroyo!"

Jasmine blushed. "Sorry. I didn't mean to yell. I just can't wait to read *Because of Winn-Dixie* to my dog!"

Suddenly, Madison's plan didn't seem so great after all. She thought about the babyish books in her backpack. They were nowhere near as hard to read as *Because of Winn-Dixie*. What if her friends saw her books and they teased her for choosing such easy ones? Or worse, what if she tried reading and she was so nervous that even those simple words wouldn't come out?

Ms. Chu ushered everyone off the bus in single file.

"I can't wait to get inside," Jasmine continued to chatter excitedly. "Everyone in our class will get to see how cool the shelter is."

Madison quietly grabbed her backpack and followed her friends and classmates into the shelter, a knot in her stomach.

"Hello, kids!" Mrs. Wallace greeted them with a wide smile. "Welcome to Rosa's Refuge." She winked at Madison and her friends. "Or for some of you, welcome back."

Mrs. Wallace gestured toward a woman in a green "Rosa's Refuge" T-shirt.

"This is June," she said. "She's one of the adult volunteers here at the shelter. She's going to help me match up everyone with a dog, so thank you in advance for being patient."

Madison beamed. Despite her nerves, it felt good to be a regular at the shelter. Many of the animals knew her scent and the sound of her voice. They were always happy to see her. She may have been the new kid at school, but she was an expert here.

While Mrs. Wallace and June paired each student with a dog, Madison waited with her friends. Even though she was nervous about the reading project, her spirits lifted when she saw all the dogs. No matter what was going on in her life, being around animals always made her feel better.

In about ten minutes, each student had been matched with a dog. Keiko was paired with an itty-bitty Chihuahua named George who looked like he was wearing the world's smallest tuxedo. He had a shiny black back, a completely white chest, and white paws to match. Sofia had gotten a white poodle with reddish eyes and a pink nose. And Jasmine had been assigned to

Roger, an older German shepherd who didn't seem pleased at all to be there. He huffed and growled and chased his own tail in circles. All their cages were side by side, but there was an empty space where one more cage should be.

"Where's my dog?" Madison asked.

"Oh yes," said Mrs. Wallace. "Your assignment is a special case. For now, we're keeping him in a separate room. Even the sound of other dogs makes him nervous, and we don't want to make it worse by surrounding him with new children as well. Once I'm done giving everyone else their instructions, you and I can go meet him."

Madison could hardly believe her luck. She wouldn't have to read or recite from memory in front of her classmates after all!

Once Mrs. Wallace had the kids settled on large pillows in front of the dogs' cages, she stepped back. "Now you've all met the dogs you'll be working with for the next few weeks. Please spend a few minutes getting to know them and letting them get to know you. Madison, would you like to tell your classmates how to say hello to a dog?"

"You can let them smell your hand from the outside of the cage for starters," Madison said helpfully. She felt giddy with relief.

"But how do I know she's not about to clamp her jaws onto my fingers?" Jimmy asked, staring at the pit bull puppy he'd been assigned.

Madison knew people tended to be afraid of pit bulls. But Madison also knew they were sweet, loyal dogs who were super affectionate if given the chance.

"You do it safely, like this." She held out her hand, palm up, just close enough to the bars of the cage to let the dog sniff her fingers.

Jimmy tried it and was rewarded with a huff and a tail wag from the puppy.

Mrs. Wallace turned to Madison. "Shall we go meet your dog?" she asked.

"Sure!" Madison agreed eagerly as she followed Mrs. Wallace into one of the exam rooms.

"You'll be working with Buddy," Mrs. Wallace said, gesturing toward a young golden retriever cowering in a cage. It was the same dog they'd met during the grand opening—the one who had been too scared to go anywhere near Mr. Brady.

"I'll be back in a minute to check on you," Mrs. Wallace said.

"Hi, Buddy," Madison said. Buddy swung his big brown eyes toward her and let out a pitiful whine.

"Aw, Buddy," Madison whispered. "I know how you feel. I was really nervous to come here today, too."

As Madison spoke softly to Buddy, she began to relax. Maybe this reading project wasn't going to be so bad after all. Buddy stayed hunched in the back of the cage, watching her and whining nervously.

After a few minutes, Mrs. Wallace returned with Ms. Chu. "How's everything?" Mrs. Wallace asked.

"I'm fine, but Buddy doesn't seem too happy," Madison replied.

Mrs. Wallace sighed. "Buddy is a very anxious dog."

"Poor puppy," said Ms. Chu. "Do you think having Madison read to him will help?"

"I hope so," Mrs. Wallace replied. "We have to get him used to people somehow, or I'm afraid no one will adopt him."

Madison gasped softly. Poor Buddy! If he didn't get over his fears, he might never find his forever home.

"Why don't you go ahead and give it a try, Madison?" Ms. Chu said encouragingly. "Maybe Buddy would like to hear a story."

"Right!" said Madison, and she opened her backpack and pulled out *The Cat in the Hat* and

Green Eggs and Ham. Even though Madison knew the words and it was just Ms. Chu, she still felt nervous. She flipped from one book to the other, trying to decide which one to read first. Finally, she chose *The Cat in the Hat.* She began to read aloud slowly at first, but she had read the book so many times that she was soon saying all the words from memory at a regular pace. Then she moved on to *Green Eggs and Ham* and read that one, too.

Ms. Chu listened quietly the entire time. But Buddy was still whining nervously. When she was done, Madison looked up at her teacher and smiled tentatively.

Her teacher smiled back, but Madison could tell right away that Ms. Chu hadn't been fooled. She sighed. Teachers were like that.

"You did a good job, Madison," Ms. Chu said gently. "But maybe next time you could choose a book that's a little more of a challenge. It would be good for you, and Buddy might find it more interesting, too."

Madison nodded. Then she looked at poor Buddy and wondered if she'd ever be able to help him.

Chapter 6:
Madison's Plan

By their next shelter visit, Madison had decided on a new plan. Maybe reading wasn't the key to getting through to her dog after all. At least, that's what she told herself as she followed her friends into the shelter.

Jasmine, Sofia, and Keiko took their seats next to their dogs while Madison waited for Mrs. Wallace to take her back to see Buddy.

Keiko had brought a book of silly poems and she dove right in, reading the first one to the Chihuahua, who simply stared at her curiously. Madison realized she was staring, too. Keiko was a great reader. She hardly ever stumbled over her words, and she never had to slow down to sound something out. Madison wondered if she would ever read that well. Soon the room was filled with the sounds of kids reading softly to the shy shelter dogs.

Finally, Mrs. Wallace came over to Madison.

"Why don't we go see Buddy now?" she asked.

"Sure," Madison agreed. Then she took a deep breath and crossed her fingers behind her back. She hoped Mrs. Wallace would think this was a great idea, too. "Would it be all right if I brought Buddy to the play room for a while?"

Mrs. Wallace's usually smooth face wrinkled as she stared at Madison through her glasses. "Oh, I'm not sure that's a good idea, Madison. Buddy has been very reluctant to leave the safety of the cage. That's why we wanted you to read to him first so that he gets comfortable with you."

"I will," Madison promised, "but I think Buddy needs a little play time first. We have to become, you know . . . buddies."

Mrs. Wallace looked thoughtful. "Well, he hasn't shown any signs of aggression, and you do seem to have a way with the animals here, so I guess it would be all right if you took him back there for a few minutes. But don't forget that you're really here to read. The project is for your benefit, too."

"Okay," Madison said. "Thanks!"

Mrs. Wallace helped her get Buddy out of his cage and into the play room. June, the shelter volunteer who had helped pair the students with their dogs on the first day of the reading project, came along, too. She stayed in the play room just in case Madison needed her.

As soon as they entered the room, Buddy ran to the nearest corner and cowered there, his ears and tail sagging.

"Aw, you don't have to be afraid of me, boy," Madison cooed. "I'm not here to hurt you. I'm your friend!" In answer, Buddy turned his head toward the wall and thumped his tail against the floor. *This won't be easy*, Madison thought.

But she'd come prepared. She unzipped her backpack and pulled out a lime-green tennis ball. "Hey, Buddy! Fetch! Fetch the ball!" she said, tossing it.

Buddy lifted his head to watch the spinning green tennis ball as it bounced against the wall and then rolled across the floor, but he didn't move a muscle to go after it. Madison picked up the ball and rolled it right at him, but that only seemed to make him more nervous. He leaped up and ran to a different corner and glared at Madison.

"Okay," said Madison. "I guess you don't like playing fetch." She reached into her bag again and pulled out a bone that was especially for young dogs. Maybe that was his problem— his teeth were bothering him and he needed something to chew on. But the bone got the same reaction as the tennis ball.

Madison glanced over at June. "Is it okay if I give Buddy a few T-R-E-A-T-S?" she asked, spelling the word in case Buddy recognized it.

June chuckled. "Sure, it's fine," she agreed. "Just don't give him *too* many."

Madison pulled out a plastic baggie that she had filled with chicken-flavored dog treats called Chicken Chewies. Madison didn't have a super-powered sense of smell like dogs did, but even she could smell the snacks before she untied the bag.

"Now, Buddy, I wouldn't usually give you treats so close to lunchtime. But I'm desperate!" She plopped a few Chicken Chewies into her palm and held her hand out toward Buddy. He sniffed at them, then turned his head away. Each time she tried to get closer, he shrank farther back.

All right, Madison thought. *If you won't let me come to you, maybe you'll come to me.*

She crept as close to Buddy as he would allow and dropped a Chicken Chewie on the floor. Then she stepped a few paces back and dropped another. She kept it up until there was a trail of Chicken Chewies dotting the floor, leading straight to Madison, who sat back on her heels, waiting patiently.

Buddy sniffed at the piece closest to him. He seemed suspicious at first, but he soon snapped up the tasty treat and gulped it down.

"That's it," Madison whispered. "Good boy."

Slowly, Buddy lapped up treat after treat, each time looking a little less scared. By the time he ate the last Chicken Chewie, he was standing right next to Madison, looking up at her with hope in his eyes. Madison held out her hand, which had one last Chicken Chewie in it. Keeping his eyes on her the whole time, Buddy carefully stuck his snout into Madison's palm, grabbed the treat between his teeth, and trotted back across the room to eat it.

Madison smiled and glanced over at June, who gave her a big smile and a thumbs-up.

Madison beamed. She knew she had started to earn Buddy's trust.

After June put Buddy back in his cage, Madison stood there proudly, thinking about what they'd just achieved.

"How did it go?" Mrs. Wallace asked when Madison returned to the rest of the class.

"It went great!" Madison said cheerfully as she gathered up her books and got ready to head out to the school bus. "Buddy let me get close to him and everything."

"Wow!" Sofia exclaimed. "That dog was so shy before! Whatever you read to him must have been really good."

"Actually, I didn't read to him at all," Madison explained. "But I think we're friends now. He even took a treat from my hand!"

"That is progress," Mrs. Wallace said. "We have had a few people interested in adopting him, but when they saw how fearful he was, they chose other dogs."

"What will happen to him if he doesn't get adopted?" Jasmine asked. "He . . . he won't be . . . put to sleep, will he?" Her voice quivered.

Mrs. Wallace patted Jasmine's shoulder comfortingly. "No, nothing like that. This is a no-kill shelter, which means Buddy can live here for as long as he needs to."

Jasmine sighed in relief.

"It's not the same, though," Mrs. Wallace added.

Madison looked up at her. "The same as what?"

"As having a family who loves him and a place he can call home."

Madison thought about how happy she and her mom were in their new home with Leo and Pepper, and how safe she felt there. Buddy deserved that, too.

She was determined to help him.

"Pass the popcorn!" Sofia yelled from one end of the couch.

"Only if you pass the Cookie," Keiko answered from the other.

Between them, Madison and Jasmine giggled as they handed the giant bowl of popcorn to Sofia, while passing not a chocolate-chip cookie, but a wiggling dachshund, back to Keiko. Now that Keiko had mostly gotten past her fear of dogs, she and Jasmine's dog, Cookie, were pals.

This was Madison's first slumber party at Jasmine's house. After they'd had dinner with Jasmine's parents, they'd played card games and watched a movie, laughing and talking through the whole thing. Now the four of them were squished together on the couch in their pajamas.

"What should we do now?" Madison asked.

"I saved the best for last," Jasmine said, jumping up. A few seconds later, she returned with a thin metal stand that had wheels on the bottom and a flat wide screen on top.

"What's that?" asked Sofia. "Don't tell me you built a robot."

Keiko giggled. "No, it's better than a robot. It's a karaoke machine!"

Jasmine smiled. "My dad just got it, and I've been dying to try it out." She flipped a switch near the base. Then she tapped a few buttons and a list appeared on the screen. "All you have to do is choose a song, and the background music starts playing."

Keiko picked up the microphone dangling from a cord on the side of the stand. "Then you sing into this, and boom, you're a star!"

"Cool!" said Sofia. She took the microphone from Keiko and struck a pose with the microphone close to her open mouth, as if she were belting out her favorite tune.

Jasmine laughed. "Well, let's start the show! Mom and Dad can be our audience."

Madison's heart sank. She knew that

karaoke involved reading the lyrics off the screen as you sang. There would be no way she could read fast enough to keep up with the song. Her friends were sure to notice, and the fun slumber party would become a nightmare. She had to do something, and fast!

"I don't know, you guys," Madison said. "Don't you want to make hot fudge sundaes instead? My mom and I brought whipped cream and everything."

"After all that popcorn I just ate?" Sofia stuck out her tongue and crossed her eyes, holding her belly. "No, thanks. If I eat one more bite, my stomach will explode!"

"Besides, even Cookie wants to sing. Look!" Keiko held up the microphone in front of

Cookie's snout, and he yipped and wagged his tail happily.

Madison sighed. Even Cookie would be no help.

"But . . . but . . . I don't think I know all the words to any songs," Madison tried.

"No problem," Sofia chimed right away. "The words pop up on the screen, too! All you have to do is read along. It's so easy."

But that was the problem. It *wasn't* easy— at least not for Madison. Why couldn't reading be as simple for her as it seemed to be for everyone else? Thinking about it made her feel like hiding in a corner, just like Buddy.

"Come on, Madison," Jasmine called, waving her closer. "Help us pick out a song."

Since she couldn't think of any more excuses, Madison joined Jasmine and the others by the karaoke machine as they skimmed through the list of song choices. They scrolled so quickly that Madison couldn't even read the names of the songs. Luckily, Jasmine started to read them out loud.

"Let's see . . . there's 'Dance Party,' 'If I Were You,' 'Friends Forever' . . ."

"Ooh, that's the one!" Madison cried. "'Friends Forever.' I love that song." She didn't mention that she knew all the words by heart.

"Great choice!" Jasmine said. "What do you think, Cookie?"

The dachshund turned in a tight circle with his long body, then wagged his tail and let out a few happy barks.

"Looks like he approves," said Sofia. "Now let's rock!"

The music started and Madison happily sang along with her friends while Jasmine's mom and dad sat on the couch and applauded. Inside, Madison breathed a sigh of relief. Once again, her secret was safe.

Chapter 8:
Cat's Out of the Bag

The next week, the four girls stood just inside the door of the shelter, excited to be back. As their classmates settled in with their dogs, Jasmine, Keiko, Sofia, and Madison stood in one corner with their backpacks.

Jasmine pulled out a copy of *Frog and Toad Are Friends*. "I saw this in the library and thought it was just perfect. Roger's going to love it! What did you guys bring?"

Keiko had brought *Charlotte's Web*, Sofia held out a well-worn copy of *Shiloh*, and then they all turned to Madison, who pulled out a plastic baggie full of dog treats.

Sofia pointed at the bag. "Bad news, Madison. Looks like your book magically turned into a bag of Chicken Chewies."

"Where's your book?" asked Jasmine.

Madison tried for a brave smile. "I don't have one."

"Did you forget it?" Keiko asked. "I'm pretty sure Ms. Chu has some extras with her."

"And my mom has a big veterinary book here. It's pretty boring, but I bet Buddy won't mind," Jasmine added.

"I have one you can borrow," said Sofia. She

reached into her backpack and pulled out a copy of *Charlie and the Chocolate Factory*. "But don't get any doggy drool on it. This is my mom's copy from when she was a kid."

"No, really. It's okay," Madison said, pushing the book back toward Sofia. "I didn't bring a book on purpose. I'm going to take Buddy to the play room again. I think it's really working."

Her three friends glanced at one another.

"Madison, you have to read to Buddy sometime," Keiko pointed out gently.

Sofia nodded. "Yeah, this is the Shelter Dog Reading Project, which means we have to read."

"I know," Madison said, frowning. "But . . . I don't want to read to him, okay?"

"Why not?" Jasmine asked. "Maybe it

would help him. Buddy is so nervous. If he doesn't improve, he'll never get adopted. You have to try everything you can to help him."

"I *am* doing everything I can," Madison replied.

"Not if you aren't reading to him," Keiko said quietly. "That's the whole point of the project, remember?"

"I *know!*" Madison cried. "I just can't! I'm not a good reader, okay?" She hadn't meant to blurt it out, but now that she had, she couldn't take it back.

Jasmine looked at her friend, a puzzled look on her face. "What do you mean?"

Madison let out a long slow breath. "I have trouble reading," she mumbled. "I have to see a reading specialist at school."

"You do?" Keiko asked. "I didn't know that. Why didn't you tell us?"

Madison lowered her head. "I was embarrassed. And reading looks so easy for you. I was afraid if you all knew how hard it was for me, you wouldn't want to be my friend anymore." Madison sniffled, holding back tears.

Jasmine hugged Madison. "I'm so sorry!" she said. "I wish you had told us so we knew what was going on. You don't have to be embarrassed."

Sofia nodded. "Yeah," she agreed. "There are a lot of things I'm not good at."

"Like what?" Madison asked, wiping her eyes.

"Well, I still haven't learned how to ride a bike," Sofia admitted.

"Really?" Madison replied. Learning to ride a bike had been easy for her. She was surprised that someone as athletic as Sofia couldn't do it.

"And I still have trouble tying my shoelaces," Keiko confessed, her cheeks turning pink. "I've practiced for ages, but I still can't get it right."

Jasmine said, "And I'm not great at sports. Just ask Sofia."

Sofia smiled at Jasmine. "She tries hard at soccer, but she has two left feet."

"The point is, we all have stuff we aren't good at, but there are things we're great at, too," Jasmine told her.

Keiko nodded. "Just look at how awesome you are with animals! You're great at so many things; you shouldn't feel bad about the one thing you need to work on."

"Correction—two things," Sofia said. "You need to trust your friends more."

Madison nodded. Maybe her friends really did know how she felt! "But . . . it takes me so long to sound out the words."

"Buddy won't care if you read slowly," Sofia pointed out. "He can't read at all!"

Everyone laughed. Madison felt relieved for the first time in weeks. "I guess you're right," she mumbled.

Jasmine handed Madison the copy of *Frog and Toad Are Friends.* "Why don't you give it a try now? You can practice on Roger."

Madison took the book. "And you're sure you won't laugh?"

"Of course not," answered Keiko. "Friends don't laugh at each other."

Sofia nodded encouragingly. "We'll all be here to help you."

Madison opened the book and, very slowly, began to read.

Chapter 9:
Being Brave

A few minutes later, Mrs. Wallace came into the room to check on everyone.

"I see you're reading to Roger," she said to Madison. "But look, Buddy's back in the main room, with the other dogs! I think your work with him really helped him adjust to being here." She gestured to the opposite corner of the room, where there was a cage off to the side that the girls hadn't noticed.

"Buddy!" Madison cried, going over to him. "I'm sorry I didn't see you there."

She settled into the cushion Mrs. Wallace had placed in front of his cage. As usual, Buddy was anxiously pacing at the back of his cage, but he wasn't whining. He watched Madison with trusting eyes as she leaned in close. "If you're brave enough to try hanging out with all these dogs again, then I'm brave enough to read to you," she whispered as she opened her book, took a deep breath, and slowly began to read aloud.

It took a while at first. Madison tried to remember the techniques her reading specialist, Ms. Patel, had taught her. She carefully sounded out each of the words, picturing the story in her mind. Every time she stumbled, she would look up, afraid she would see her classmates pointing and laughing at her. But no one was even listening to her. They were all concentrating on their own books.

By the time Madison had finished the first page, she felt more confident. But the best part was that Buddy had inched closer to the front of the cage, and his ears had perked up.

"Look!" Keiko whispered, careful not to scare Buddy off. "It's working!"

"Nice job," Sofia said, patting Madison on the back.

"Way to go!" Jasmine added with an encouraging smile.

Madison beamed. After that, reading got a little easier. Madison focused on making Buddy feel less afraid, and she felt braver, too. Not only did she sound out the words a little faster, but she acted out the different characters and stopped to show Buddy the pictures, too. By the time the class headed back to school that day, Madison was feeling great.

Two weeks later, Madison was back at the shelter on a Saturday volunteering with her friends. As soon as she walked in the door, she ran over to Buddy to say hello. He was standing at the front of his cage, wagging his tail and panting softly. He seemed so much happier, Madison could hardly believe it.

"Hi, girls!" Mrs. Wallace said brightly. Then she smiled at Madison. "I see Buddy's happy to see his best friend today. He's been doing so well lately. He's gained a tiny bit of weight, and he even let me trim his nails and brush his teeth yesterday."

"Wow!" Madison said as she raised her hand to the cage so Buddy could smell her. She was surprised when he gave her fingers a friendly lick.

"You're a miracle worker, Madison," Mrs. Wallace said. "He's improved so much since you started working with him."

"Thanks," said Madison, flushing with pride. "Do you think someone will adopt him now?"

"Oh yes, I think so," said Mrs. Wallace. "Because of you, Buddy is sure to find a good family to take him in. And whoever takes him home now is going to have to read him a bedtime story every night!"

Chapter 10:
An Unlikely Hero

A few days later, Madison and her friends were in class on an ordinary Tuesday afternoon, but the day was hardly ordinary. They were having a pizza party!

"I told you we could win!" Jasmine cried as she lifted a slice of pepperoni pizza out of the large cardboard box and slid it onto her paper plate.

"I never doubted it for a second," Sofia chimed in.

"Mmm . . . extra cheese," mumbled Keiko as she took a big bite of her slice.

Madison smiled to herself as she watched her friends dig in. Facing her fears and coming through for her friends—and for Buddy—was better than even the most delicious slice of pizza.

Suddenly, Mr. Brady appeared at the door. "Hello, Ms. Chu. Mind if I join the party for a moment? I just wanted to congratulate this class on a job well done. You should be very proud."

Everyone cheered.

"I've heard from Mrs. Wallace at the shelter," Mr. Brady went on. "She told me that several of the dogs you worked with have been adopted or will be soon. In fact, the Shelter Dog

Reading Project was so successful that they might do it again next year."

"That's wonderful news, Mr. Brady," Ms. Chu said with a huge smile.

"Yeah, it's awesome!" Madison cried happily. "If they need volunteers to read to them again, sign me up!"

"Me too!" shouted Keiko.

"Me three!" said Jasmine.

"Me four!" finished Sofia.

Madison gave each of her friends a high five.

Mr. Brady grinned. "I'm glad you all feel that way, because I've brought some surprise guests with me who want to celebrate, too. Come on in, Mrs. Wallace!"

Madison shared a pleased grin with Jasmine. They'd both been so excited to show everyone at school around the shelter. Now Mrs. Wallace would get to see their school!

Madison's grin widened when she saw that Mrs. Wallace hadn't come alone. She was holding a leash, and Madison knew the dog at the end of it very well.

"Buddy!" she exclaimed, jumping up from her chair. As soon as he heard her voice, Buddy wagged his tail happily and tugged against his leash. Madison put down her pizza and hurried over. She kneeled in front of him so she could ruffle his golden fur while he rested one paw on her leg and licked her cheek.

"Well, somebody's very happy to see you," Mrs. Wallace said with a chuckle.

"I'm happy to see him, too," Madison answered. "Has he been adopted?"

"Actually," said Mr. Brady, "I'm taking Buddy home today. Yesterday he met my wife and son, and they were just as smitten with him as I was."

Madison hugged Buddy around his scruffy neck and whispered, "Good boy! Congratulations."

After Mr. Brady left, Ms. Chu announced that it was time to read their stories of inspiration out loud. "And now we'll have an even bigger audience!" She gestured to Mrs. Wallace and Buddy. "Who would like to go first?"

Surprising herself, Madison's hand shot into the air.

"Wonderful," said Ms. Chu. "The floor is yours."

As Madison made her way to the front, she started to get cold feet. The class looked so much bigger from up there! Just when she started to think maybe this wasn't such a good idea after all, her gaze fell on her three friends. Keiko smiled from ear to ear, Jasmine gave her two thumbs up, and Sofia mouthed "you can do it!"

Madison smiled, looked down at her story, and slowly began to read. "The person who has inspired me the most isn't ac-actually a person. I've always had tr-trouble reading, and I needed help." She paused to see if there would be any reaction to her big reveal and her stuttering, or any laughter or pointed fingers. But there wasn't. Even Eddie, the class clown, sat quietly.

"When I f-first came to this school, I was afraid people would find out about my pr-pr-problem and not want to be my friend. I was so sc-scared by the Shelter Dog Reading Project. But then I met a puppy named Buddy.

"Buddy was just as scared as I was. But in a way, that made me feel less ner-nervous." Madison described how she and Buddy had become friends, and how reading to him had helped her build up her confidence. Then she described how Keiko, Jasmine, and Sofia had encouraged her to be brave and read aloud at the shelter. "They told me to do it for Buddy, so I did—and now I love to read, thanks to him!" she finished.

"Great job, Madison," Ms. Chu said. "Thank you for volunteering to go first." Everyone clapped loudly, and Madison smiled at her friends. Thanks to them—and to her new friend, Buddy—she felt like she could overcome any challenge. Madison knew she would always have three great friends by her side, helping her until she succeeded.

CRYSTAL VELASQUEZ was born in the Bronx, New York. She studied English and creative writing at Pennsylvania State University and is a graduate of NYU's Summer Publishing Institute. She lives in Flushing, New York, and hopes to adopt a new puppy very soon.

Don't miss the next  book!

Keiko's Pony Rescue

When Keiko's aunt invites her and her friends Madison, Jasmine, and Sofia to spend two weeks on her farm, the girls are thrilled. They can't wait to milk a cow and take care of all the farm animals, including a horse who's expecting a baby! But when the foal is born with a leg problem, the girls aren't sure how to help. Will the new foal be okay?

A group of girls so close, they're just

Like Sisters

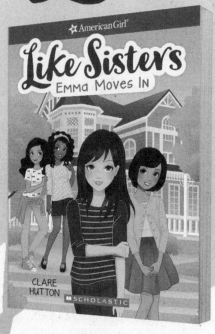

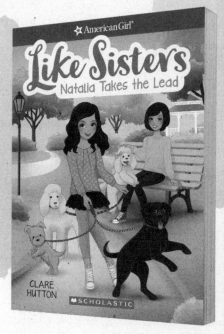

Emma loves visiting her twin cousins, Natalia and Zoe, so she's thrilled when her family moves to their town after living 3,000 miles away. Emma knows her life is about to change in a big way. And it will be more wonderful and challenging than any of the girls expect!

There's going to be a wedding at the inn—with dog ring bearers! Natalia loves dogs and offers to watch and walk them. But has Natalia bitten off more than she can chew? When one of the dogs goes missing, Natalia enlists Emma, Caitlin, and Zoe to help. If they can't find the dog, the wedding will be wrecked!

⭐ American Girl

📕 SCHOLASTIC